The
Reveres:
A Family Forced Apart

Suzanne Lieurance

TIPS FOR REHEARSING READER'S THEATER

BY AARON SHEPARD

- Make sure your script doesn't hide your face. If there is anyone in the audience you can't see, your script is too high.

- While you speak, try to look up often. Don't just look at your script. When you do look at the script, move just your eyes and keep your head up.

- Talk slowly. Speak each syllable clearly.

- Talk loudly! You have to be heard by every person in the room.

- Talk with feeling. Your voice has to tell the story.

- Stand or sit up straight. Keep your hands and feet still if they're doing nothing useful.

- If you're moving around, face the audience as much as you can. When rehearsing, always think about where the audience will be.

- Characters, remember to be your character even when you're not speaking.

- Narrators, make sure you give the characters enough time for their actions.

TIPS FOR PERFORMING READER'S THEATER

BY AARON SHEPARD

- If the audience laughs, stop speaking until they can hear you again.

- If someone talks in the audience, don't pay attention.

- If someone walks into the room, don't look at him or her.

- If you make a mistake, pretend it was right.

- If you drop something, try to leave it where it is until the audience is looking somewhere else.

- If a reader forgets to read his or her part, see if you can read the part instead, make something up, or just skip over it. Don't whisper to the reader!

- If a reader falls down during the performance, pretend it didn't happen.

THE REVERES: A FAMILY FORCED APART

Characters

Narrator   **Debby Revere**

Rachel Revere   **Sarah Revere**

Paul Revere, Jr.   **Thomas Green**

Setting

This reader's theater takes place in April and May of 1775, in Boston, Massachusetts. This story is based on actual events.

Rachel Revere   Paul Revere, Jr.   Debby Revere   Sarah Revere   Thomas Green

Act 1

Narrator:	It is the morning of April 19, 1775. Paul Revere, Jr., and two of his five sisters are awake early. Rachel is preparing breakfast while Sarah tends to the baby.
Rachel:	Sarah, get your sisters up and ready for school.

Sarah: But Father hasn't returned yet. How can we go to school when we don't know if he's safe?

Rachel: Most people don't realize where your father went last night. Let them think things are no different for us today than they were yesterday.

Narrator: Sarah leaves the room to go wake her younger sisters.

Paul: I should stick to my routine and go to Father's silver shop today as usual, too. People will expect me to be working there as always. But I do wish we would receive word from Father first.

Debby: We'll hear from him soon enough. Here, eat your breakfast. Where did Father go this time, Mother?

Narrator: Rachel puts plates of food on the table. Sarah comes back into the room.

Rachel: Your father was sent on a very dangerous mission. As you know, the king of England has made life miserable for the colonists for a long time.

Paul: He certainly has! Many colonists are tired of paying such high taxes on goods. And now that British soldiers occupy Boston and have blockaded the port, many people grow angrier every day.

Rachel: These angry rebels have started to form small troops called militias. The rebels are prepared for possible war with England.

Sarah: But what does Father have to do with any of this? He is a silversmith, a master craftsman.

Rachel: He is also a messenger for the rebels, the Sons of Liberty.

Debby: But the king has messengers, too. He knows the rebels have been storing weapons and ammunition in Concord. Last night, the king sent British soldiers to seize those weapons. He thought the rebels would be too afraid to fight the British regulars. After all, the rebel soldiers we call minutemen are only farmers, shop owners, and simple slaves. How can they be as strong as the well-trained British regulars?

Paul: Do you mean that Father was sent to Concord last night to warn the colonists the British regulars were coming?

Rachel: Yes, I do.

Debby: Do you think the regulars have captured Father and that is why he has not returned?

Rachel: Certainly not, my dear. But he cannot return to Boston now. The regulars would throw him in jail.

Narrator: There's a knock at the door. The children look worried.

Paul: Who goes there?

Thomas: It is only I, your friend and neighbor, Thomas Green. Let me in, Paul.

Narrator: Paul opens the door. A boy about his age removes his hat and comes in.

Thomas: Good morning, all. I'm sorry to disturb your breakfast. But I bring you news. Everyone is talking about Mr. Revere and the courageous ride he took last night to warn the colonists about the regulars. He made it to Lexington, where Mr. Adams and Mr. Hancock were hiding. He got there just in time to help them escape before they could be captured.

Sarah: Why would the regulars want Mr. Adams and Mr. Hancock?

Paul: Because, silly girl, they are Patriots who want the colonies to break away from England to form their own country. The king wants them arrested and thrown into jail.

Thomas: Mr. Adams and Mr. Hancock have been organizing militias throughout the colonies so we can fight the British. The king thinks their capture will keep the militias from fighting. But the fighting has already started. It began early this morning in Lexington. Scores of minutemen where there. Women and children, too, I hear, to load muskets and tend to the wounded. So many minutemen were there, in fact, that as the British were retreating from Concord, they were defeated.

Sarah: That's good news! But, what will happen to our father now? Where will he go?

Thomas:	My father says it will probably be months before Paul Revere can show his face in Boston again. The British will be watching for him, so they have to leave the city before your father can return.
Debby:	Oh, dear! That could be months from now. I don't want to even think about life without Father.
Paul:	Well, we can't just sit here and fret. I'm sure we'll have an encouraging message from Father soon. In the meantime, we will do as Mother says—carry on, as usual.

Poem: Carrying On

Act 2

Narrator:	The next day after school, Sarah rushes into the house. She finds her mother at her desk, holding a letter. Debby is standing beside her mother.
Sarah:	Is that a letter from Father? Is he safe?

Rachel:	Yes, your father is well. You needn't worry any longer.
Debby:	Father is well. But he needs clothes and money for food and other necessities.
Narrator:	Paul and Thomas enter the house.
Rachel:	I must write to him and send money. Doctor Church will see that your father receives it.
Paul:	Did I hear you say that you plan to give Dr. Church a letter with money to take to Father? Are you sure you can trust Dr. Church?
Thomas:	He might be a member of the Sons of Liberty, but many think he is also a spy for the British.
Rachel:	I don't know about that. For now, we have to trust him. Children, as soon as this letter is sent, we must get ready to join your father. It will take time to prepare.
Narrator:	Later that day, Dr. Church comes to the Revere home. Rachel gives him the letter. She doesn't know that Dr. Church pockets the money after he leaves. He turns the letter over to General Gage, a British general. As a result, there is word later that the British have captured Paul Revere, along with others. Sometime later, Rachel receives another letter from her husband.

Rachel:	Father has been released and he wants us to join him! He says he can't return to Boston yet, lest he be arrested or otherwise bring trouble to our home. First, he wants us to send furniture and household belongings.
Paul:	What else does Father's letter say?
Rachel:	He says, "Come with the children, except Paul. Pray order him by all means to keep at home that he may help bring the things to the ferry. Tell him not to come till I send for him."

Debby: I don't understand. Why does Paul need to stay here? What purpose could that possibly serve?

Paul: I know why. Father talked to me about this weeks ago. Look outside. Haven't you noticed what's happening here? The regulars are hungry and cold. They need food and wood for their campfires. When they find a house unoccupied, they take any food they find. They use the furniture to build their campfires.

Debby: How horrible! I would hate for the regulars to take our valuable belongings and ruin our home.

Paul: Don't worry. The British will not trespass into our home and disturb our property. I will see to that. But what will I do for food while I am here alone? And who will cook, wash my clothes, and tend to the house?

Debby: Don't be a ninny, Paul. You will be industrious. You will simply hunt and fish for your food. And before we go, we will teach you how to cook and clean for yourself.

Paul: Nonsense! Cooking and cleaning are women's work. Men were made for more courageous tasks.

Debby: Women's work, huh? Then feast on raw meat and wear dirty clothes for all I care!

Sarah: But I insist you learn to keep the house clean. We can't come home to a pigsty!

Rachel: Girls, let Paul be. Food will be scarce in the markets now that the war has started. So, you will probably need to hunt and fish for much of your food, Paul. As for more courageous tasks, it will take great courage to fend for yourself.

Thomas: Don't worry, girls! I'll be here to help Paul whenever he needs me. We already hunt and fish together. In fact, we have two large fish outside in a bucket. We caught them this very afternoon.

Paul: That's right. We do. They will make a hearty supper.

Debby: Indeed, they will, if cooked properly. But we will need more for supper than fish.

Thomas:	Then we'll make a fish pie with plenty of vegetables.
Sarah:	Ha! Fish pie is Paul's favorite. But I know for a fact that he does not have the slightest idea how to make it.
Thomas:	But I do. I've watched my mother and sisters prepare fish pie many times.
Narrator:	Paul and Thomas shoo the girls out of the kitchen so they can make fish pie. After awhile, the boys call them back for supper. The kitchen is a mess. Flour is everywhere. Sarah stares at the fish pie.
Sarah:	Is that disgusting looking concoction supposed to be our supper?
Paul:	Yes. But it doesn't look disgusting. It looks delicious. Try it.
Debby:	Why don't you try it yourself if it appears so appetizing to your eyes? It looks rather revolting to mine.
Thomas:	Move away, you cowards. I will taste it myself.
Narrator:	Thomas takes a bite of the fish pie, but he immediately runs for the door. He spits the bite of pie outside.
Paul:	It can't be that bad.
Thomas:	I'm afraid it can be, Paul. I'd say our fish pie is foul.

Narrator: The girls giggle.

Debby: Make up your minds, gentlemen. Is your pie—fish or fowl?

Rachel: Enough teasing, Debby. You and I will make supper. Tomorrow we will teach Paul to make a proper fish pie.

Act 3

Narrator: For several weeks, Rachel and the girls teach Paul how to cook, how to care for his clothes, and how to clean the house.

Rachel: Girls, it is time for us to join your father. Pack everything in a basket, Debby. We must all get the cart ready for our journey.

Narrator:	Rachel and the girls pile a straw mattress onto a small cart. They hide food under the mattress. Paul hitches their father's horse, named Militia, to the cart just as Rachel arrives home with the pass. She gathers the family and a few more belongings.
Rachel:	I think we are ready. It is time to go. Paul, you are the man of the house now. Look after it well.

Act 4

Narrator:	Meanwhile, Mr. Paul Revere realizes that his family will not be safe in Boston, and that he will surely be arrested if he appears there. So he sends his family to lodging just a few miles outside of town, where they hide for 11 months. Paul Jr. and other teenage boys are left to guard homes of Patriots.
Thomas:	Paul, I wasn't able to catch any fish today. Why don't we try the slingshots? I saw so many squirrels in the tree right over there. That way we can both hunt at the same time, and also guard our homes.
Paul:	I am so tired of squirrel! I never thought I'd miss my sisters' cooking so much.
Thomas:	When I was down at the pier trying to catch us some dinner, I heard that the Gilbert's house was ransacked!
Paul:	Oh no, not another one! And I heard that regulars moved into the school house and they are burning desks to keep warm at night. We must be extra careful. They seem to be running out of places to ransack.

Thomas:	Why can't they collect firewood every morning like we have to?
Paul:	I am just glad I don't have to fight them for the firewood. I have no weapons and they do.
Thomas:	That reminds me, when it was my turn to collect the firewood, I found a bush just full of berries! I took as many as I could fit in my pockets. We can have some with our squirrel for dinner tonight.
Paul:	Did you see that? I almost had him! Berries may be the only things we will have for dinner tonight! I am so hungry!
Thomas:	Paul! I think someone is looking in the windows of your house! There, on the other side! I will watch from here. You go run inside and make some noise and build up your fire, too!

Narrator: Paul nervously runs inside and throws more wood on the fire. He stomps around a bit until the regulars run off. Paul peers out a window and then stands in the doorway and looks around. When he sees that it is safe, he goes back to the tree.

Paul: This is so hard! I used to think it was hard to work in my father's shop. Now it seems like it would be a fun thing to do.

Thomas: I got one! We have roast squirrel for dinner tonight!

Narrator: Both boys seem to forget their manly burdens for a moment and jump up and down. Thomas picks up the squirrel and the two of them march happily toward the house.

Thomas: After a dinner of roast squirrel and berries, we can play marbles.

Paul:	Thomas, do you think that the regulars might run out of food and firewood soon? Do you suppose that when they do, they will smell our fish or even this squirrel and come ransack us?
Thomas:	How can we know what will happen? We just have to be brave, don't you think? When our families return they will be so glad to see that we have saved our homes. That's all I can think about. Here, help me get this squirrel ready.
Paul:	My sisters will be so surprised when they find out I can cook squirrel pie, squirrel roast, and squirrel soup!

 Song: Squirrel Pie

Act 5

Narrator:	Meanwhile, the Revere family is comfortable, but anxious.
Debby:	I sure hope Paul has not starved himself to death!
Sarah:	I hope our house is still there.
Debby:	Do you think the bed has been turned into firewood?
Sarah:	What if they capture Paul?
Rachel:	I worry for him, too. I do hope he is managing. He has such a large responsibility. But he is a brave lad. I must trust that all is well.
Debby:	Father says that we can go home in a few more months.

Sarah:	I never knew that I could ever miss him this much. I even miss his disgusting fish pie! I so hope he has not starved himself. I picture him lost and hungry.
Rachel:	Paul is like his father. He will be just fine.
Narrator:	After 11 months, the family packs to return home, not knowing what they will find. Paul has not heard from his family, nor have they heard from him. When they return to Boston, they find that many buildings have been damaged. They are relieved to see that their home is still standing. They are even more relieved when they see a tired and thin, but well Paul emerge from the house to run to them. First Paul hugs his father, who whispers praises in his ear. Paul Revere appears much relieved. Next, Rachel throws her arms around her son.
Rachel:	I knew you could do it. You have become a brave man, much like your father.
Narrator:	Sarah and Debby stare at their brother. They seem to realize that he is not the boy they last saw, but a man. Then they both climb down from the wagon and race to hug him.
Paul:	Easy there! I have a bit of an injury to this arm!
Sarah:	What happened? Did the regulars wound you while you were defending our home?
Paul:	Um well . . .

Debby: I just know it was because you were brave and kept them away. Is the bed still there? Did they ever get in at all?

Paul: Well, actually . . .

Thomas: Squirrel pie is ready!

Debby: Squirrel pie? I don't think I'll be having any, thank you.

Thomas: Oh, we've perfected squirrel pie, but if you'd rather not, there'd be more for the rest of us.

Narrator: And so, the Reveres gratefully return to their home. Paul and his son return to their work, casting church bells. For the rest of his life, Paul Jr. perfects his art as a silversmith. As for the injury to Paul's arm—he snapped his slingshot and when he lost his grip, it snapped him on the arm, leaving a large welt that took a week and a half to heal.

CARRYING ON

There's work to be done while Father is gone,
Alone here at home, we must carry on.
We've got our own work, and a purpose, too.
Father's counting on us to see it through.

We'll manage the house, the chores, and the shop.
Just like him, we won't waver or stop.
When he returns, he'll be proud to find
A stronger family than he left behind.

Father's not here, but we must stand strong,
Work hard, be smart, and get along.
We'll pull together and make him see
That we're also fighting for liberty.

SQUIRREL PIE

What's for supper young Paul Revere
You're making dinner it does appear
What'cha gonna make each boy and girl
I'll bet you a penny it's gonna be squirrel

Squirrel pie, a pigeon or a hare
Put the plates on the table, it's a simple fare
Maybe it's a fish or a berry or two
Whatever we can find we're gonna have to
make do

When you're family is gone you've got to make your
own way
Trust all is well and they'll be home someday
You've got to keep your courage and a watchful eye
And you've got to make a meal of a squirrel pie

Squirrel pie, a pigeon or a hare
Put the plates on the table, it's a simple fare
Maybe it's a fish or a berry or two
Whatever we can find we're gonna have to make do
I wish that I could cook like my sisters do
But for now a squirrel pie is gonna have to do

GLOSSARY

ammunition—bullets, cannonballs, and other materials that can be fired from guns or cannons

blockade—ships used to block the entrance to a harbor or port, so the city cannot sell or receive goods

bribe—money secretly paid in exchange for something else

colonist—a person who moved from England to America but remained under the rule of England

colony—an area of land that is settled by people from another country who remain under the rule of that country. At the start of the American Revolution there were 13 colonies in America

industrious—hard-working; clever or skillful

militia—a group of citizens trained to fight in times of emergency only

minutemen—soldiers who promised to be ready to fight at a minute's notice during the early days of the Revolutionary War. Many farmers, slaves, and shop owners were minutemen.

Patriot—an American colonist who wanted independence from Britain

rebel—a colonist who fought or plotted against the British government

regulars—British foot soldiers during the American Revolution; also called Redcoats

silversmith—a person who makes or repairs items made of silver

Sons of Liberty—a rebel group of colonists that formed to fight against the taxes imposed on the colonists by the English Parliament